Hair in the Air

D0104491

Read other

SPENCER'S *adventures*

SPENCER'S adventures

Hair in the Air

by

Gary Hogg

illustrated by Chuck Slack

A
LITTLE APPLE
PAPERBACK

SCHOLASTIC INC.
New York   Toronto   London   Auckland   Sydney

ISBN 0-590-93937-8

12 11 10 9 8 7 6 5 4 3 2   7 8 9/9 0 1 2/0

Printed in the U.S.A.   40

First Scholastic printing, January 1997

For my son Jackson,
a boy whose adventures
never cease to inspire me.

CONTENTS

• • • • • • • • • • • • •

Hair in the Air

Chapter One

Pythons for Pennies

Spencer was bored. It was supposed to be a great day. Grandpa Gibson had promised to take him fishing at Milner Dam.

The last time they went there Spencer had great luck. They didn't catch any fish, but Spencer came home with a snake that he sold for 37¢ to Josh Porter. He told Josh it was a baby python.

Ever since then, Spencer had been planning the next fishing trip. He was going to leave the fishing to Grandpa and concentrate on catching snakes. He planned to catch forty or fifty snakes and sell them as baby pythons for 37¢ each. He already had an advertising slogan, "Pythons for pennies."

But now the trip was off. Grandpa had been called in to work and Spencer was stuck at Grandpa and Grandma's house. He was stuck and bored. They didn't have cable TV. They didn't have video games. They didn't have anything. Well, they did have a cat and a dog.

Barkley was a fat hunk of a dog. Grandpa called him an English sitter. That's because he liked to sit around so much. If he wasn't sitting, he was eating. His appetite was huge.

Being a great hunting dog, Barkley always killed what he was going to eat,

Pythons for Pennies
BUY A Snake
MOMS ♡ SNAKES
GREAt Pets
KEEPS GiRLS AWAY

even though it was already dead. He had killed more dishes of dog food than any other dog on the planet.

He would growl and circle and then, with teeth bared, dive in for the kill. Once he even killed one of Grandpa's slippers before eating half of it.

Snickers was a Siamese cat. He was a Siamese who thought he was a ninja. Spencer didn't like Snickers and Snickers didn't like Spencer. They were enemies. They attacked each other every chance they got.

Chapter Two

Cat Attack

Spencer stretched out on the couch. He figured since he didn't have anything else to do, he would work on growing taller.

First he relaxed and thought long thoughts of ropes, spaghetti, and worms being pulled from the ground. Then, in one sudden jerk, his body went stiff. With every muscle, he pulled on his bones to make them just a little longer.

It was while he was in this stretched-out position that Snickers spotted him. The cat took his best shot. With outstretched paws, he dive-bombed onto Spencer's belly.

Whoosh! The weight of the pouncing cat forced the air out of Spencer. He tried to yell "Cat attack!" but just a whisper whimpered out. And then suddenly, with a gasp, air flooded back into Spencer and the chase was on.

It was Snickers in the lead followed by Spencer. And around the magazine rack they went.

It was Snickers ahead by two lengths. Spencer was coming on strong as they rounded the bend and headed into the kitchen. The cat scrambled under the table and behind the chair.

They were neck and neck as they entered the home stretch. It looked like it was going to be a photo finish.

Suddenly Snickers disappeared into Grandpa and Grandma's bedroom. Spencer had never been into Grandpa's bedroom before. He was not allowed. But he had to get the cat.

Grandpa would understand. After all, the cat had taken a cheap shot. Grandpa wouldn't want him to get away with something as dirty as that. Slowly, Spencer entered the room. He would just get the cat and get out.

"Here, Snickers," said Spencer. "Come to your pal Spence. I have a little surprise for you."

Spencer looked in the closet. "Kitty, kitty, kitty." Spencer looked under the bed. "Kitty, kitty, kitty." Spencer looked behind the chair. "Kitty, kitty, kitty." Spencer looked everywhere. Finally he shouted, "Where are you, you crazy cat?"

And as Spencer turned around, there

it was. It was brown. It was hairy. It was Grandpa's toupee.

A toupee is a wig. But Grandpa wouldn't let anyone call it a wig. "Wigs are for women," he would always say.

Grandpa called his hair a rug. He said he didn't wear it because he was bald. He wore it to keep his head warm. Sometimes it kept his head so warm that he would sweat. Once he sweated so much that his rug slid right off his head.

Spencer had seen Grandpa without his hair many times. But this was the first time he had ever seen Grandpa's hair without Grandpa.

"I have always wanted to touch this," said Spencer as he poked the toupee.

It feels kind of crusty and stiff. He must use staples or tape to keep it on, thought Spencer. Then he remembered the time he stuck a staple into his finger.

Boy, did that hurt. "I'll bet he uses tape," said Spencer.

Spencer lifted up Grandpa's hair and placed it on his head. He looked in the mirror, pretending he was Grandpa. He began to say things he wished Grandpa would say.

"Spencer, you are my favorite grandson. I hate your sister. Here's fifty dollars and the car keys. Go and have some fun."

Then Spencer started to laugh. He laughed so hard that he doubled over and the toupee fell off of his head.

Chapter Three

Hairball Olympics

As Spencer reached for the toupee, Snickers suddenly appeared. He began pawing at the wig.

"Oh, you like Grandpa's hair," said Spencer. He shook the toupee faster and faster in front of Snickers.

Snickers' paws worked like lightning trying to snag the toupee. "Hey, wait a minute," said Spencer. "I have an idea for a great game."

He went over to Grandma's knitting basket, cut off a piece of brown yarn, and tied it to the toupee.

Then Spencer called out, "Ladies and gentlemen, welcome to the Hairball Olympics. First event is hairball boxing.

"In this corner, wearing furball trunks, weighing three pounds, we have Snickers the Ninja Cat.

"And in this corner, wearing nothing but hairspray, weighing half a pound, we have Grandpa's hair.

"At the sound of the bell, come out fighting. Ding. Ding."

Spencer took hold of the yarn and began bouncing the hair up and down. Snickers batted at the toupee until his claw stuck in the wig. He pulled out a paw full of hair.

"That's cheating," yelled Spencer. "No hair-pulling allowed. The cat loses the match."

Spencer grabbed one of Grandma's gold earrings and snapped it on the toupee. "The first gold medal goes to Grandpa's hair."

"Next event is the 100-yard hair dash," said Spencer, glancing around the bedroom. The room was too small for a good race. Spencer grabbed Snickers and the wig and headed out into the back yard.

"In lane number one we have Snickers the Streak. And in lane number two, we have Hairy the Toupee. On your mark. Get set. Go!" Spencer started dragging the toupee, with Snickers close behind.

Grandpa's hair flew around the flower bed. It snagged in the shrubs. It splashed through a mud puddle. And, finally, it landed in Barkley's doggie dish.

"And Hairy wins by a hair," yelled Spencer. He fell down on the grass laughing.

Snickers was tired of the Hairball Olympics. He went to the back porch and licked his paws.

"What a sore loser," Spencer told the cat.

Chapter Four

The Great Hair Scare

The sound of the slamming door startled Spencer. It came from Turner's house. Spencer remembered the time that Grandpa and Mrs. Turner got into a fight.

Grandpa was outside cooking on the grill. "The secret to a perfect barbecue is to get the fire good and hot," he said. So Grandpa created a fire that would melt steel.

It was so hot that he couldn't even get close to it. He had to stand back several feet and throw the meat at the grill. The hot dogs went up in smoke the instant they hit Grandpa's inferno. A huge cloud of smoke billowed off of the grill.

There was so much smoke that Mrs. Turner was sure that Grandpa's house was burning to the ground. She immediately called the fire department. "Hurry," she cried. "There are two old people trapped inside a burning house next door."

When Grandpa heard the sirens he said, "Do you hear that sound, Spencer? That is the sound of some very brave men risking their lives to save someone else's life and property."

He didn't know that it was his life and his hot dogs they were on their way to save.

The firemen raced into the yard dragging a long hose. They saw all the smoke coming off the grill and started to spray. The blast tipped Grandpa's barbecue over, and the smoldering wieners went rolling around on the ground.

"What on earth are you doing?" shouted Grandpa.

"We had a report of a fire at this address," said the fire chief.

"Who is crazy enough to get all worked up over a few smoking hot dogs?" demanded Grandpa.

"The call came from next door," said the firemen, pointing at Mrs. Turner's house.

There, standing on the porch was Mrs. Turner. Grandpa marched straight through the flower bed right up to his neighbor.

"Have you lost your mind?" shouted Grandpa.

"You should be thanking me," said

Mrs. Turner. "You could have been killed."

"Lady, it will take more than a couple of burning hot dogs to kill me. Take some advice and keep your big nose out of my business."

"Listen, you old coot," snapped Mrs. Turner. "You keep the smoke from your hot dogs in your own yard or next time I will call the police instead of the fire department. Now get off my property."

That was the last time that Mrs. Turner and Grandpa had spoken. Grandpa always said that he would get even.

Spencer decided that since Grandpa hadn't had time to even the score, he would let Grandpa's hair have a crack at it.

Spencer stuffed the hair down his shirt. So this is what it feels like to have hair on your chest, thought Spencer.

He sneaked into Mrs. Turner's yard on

his belly. He hid in a shrub and looked around. There was no sign of Terrible Turner.

As he crawled past the kitchen window he heard singing. "Pay dirt," said Spencer. He climbed into the cherry tree and looked in the kitchen window. Mrs. Turner was standing at the sink washing her dishes.

Spencer wrapped the yarn that was tied to the toupee around a long stick. The wig dangled down like a fish that had just been caught.

Slowly, Spencer moved the toupee in front of the window and began bouncing it up and down. The scream that Mrs. Turner let out was so loud, it made Spencer jump and he fell out of the tree.

As Spencer scrambled to get to his feet, he could hear the frightened lady screaming into the phone.

"Giant hairy spiders are attacking my

house. There is a tarantula the size of a goat looking in my kitchen window right now. Hurry. The last time I looked it was licking its big spider lips. It's hungry and it wants me."

Spencer ran back to Grandpa's yard and plopped down. "Giant hairy spiders are attacking my house," he said, laughing and holding his stomach.

Then he looked at the wig and said, "I can see why Grandpa likes you so much. For being just a hunk of hair, you are a lot of fun."

Chapter Five

Operation: Hair Rescue

Spencer started swinging Grandpa's hair around his head. It made a whirling sound. As he spun the hair faster and faster, the sound grew louder and louder.

"And now for your listening pleasure," announced Spencer, "I am proud to present Wiggy the Singing Hair. The first song he will be performing will be *I Left My Hair in San Francisco*." Spencer swung the hair faster.

Suddenly Spencer lost his grip on the yarn and the toupee went flying through the air. "Wow," he said. "Look at that hair fly."

That gave Spencer an idea for a new game. He called it "Hair in the Air."

Spencer twirled the toupee and threw it high in the air. As it flew he yelled, "Hair in the air!"

Higher and higher he sent the hair into the air. "Here comes the Hairship Enterprise," shouted Spencer.

He launched the toupee time after time. Then it happened. Grandpa's hair didn't come back. It was stuck on a branch in the old elm tree.

"Hmmm," said Spencer. "It looks like a big hairy bird nest up there." Sure enough, a bird came and landed right on top of Grandpa's toupee.

"Get out of my grandpa's hair,"

screamed Spencer. "If you have an accident on that hair, you'll be sorry."

Spencer had to rescue Grandpa's toupee. He jumped up and grabbed the first branch. He swung his feet up to the second and pulled himself up with his legs.

Now that he was in the tree, he just had to go higher. He crossed through the fork in the trunk and started up.

As he reached for the fourth branch, he felt something slick. "Oh, gross," said Spencer as he looked at his hand. His palm was covered with white goo. He looked up at the bird and yelled, "I hate your guts!" Spencer wiped his hand on his pants and kept climbing.

Soon he was higher than he had ever climbed before. The branches were smaller and didn't feel very strong.

Spencer swallowed hard and kept going. If he was going to fall and die, he was sure that everyone would understand. After all, he was on a rescue mission. His tombstone would read, "Here lies a brave boy. He died saving his grandfather's hair."

Finally Spencer reached the branch that held the toupee. He slowly started out on the limb. It began to sag with his weight.

Suddenly he felt a thud on his back. Snickers' sharp claws pierced his skin.

"Not now, you stupid cat," screamed Spencer. "You are going to kill us both."

The branch swayed back and forth. Spencer held on with one arm and tried to slug the cat with the other.

All at once, Spencer spun around on the limb. He quickly locked his legs and arms around the skinny branch. He was hanging upside down in the tree.

Snickers climbed from the branch to

Spencer's belly. "Scram, cat," shouted Spencer. Snickers stood up and began licking Spencer on the neck.

"Stop that," insisted Spencer. "You know I'm ticklish."

Spencer started to laugh. He couldn't help it. And as he giggled, he began to lose his grip on the tree. He was going to fall at any moment.

Suddenly Snickers stopped. He had spotted the toupee. He walked over Spencer's face and out to the wig. With one swift swat, he knocked the toupee out of the tree.

Chapter Six

You Dumb Dog

Spencer turned his head and watched the toupee fall to the ground. After it landed, he inched his way back to a larger branch and took hold.

When he looked down again, Barkley was standing over the toupee. He was growling.

"Don't get any ideas, Barkley," yelled Spencer. "I'm coming down."

But Barkley already had some ideas.

"RRRRRR, *what are you doing in my yard?*" demanded Barkley.

No answer from the hair.

"RRRRRR, *oh, a wise guy,*" said Barkley. *"I know how to handle you."*

The fight was a wild one. Barkley snapped up the hair in his slimy jaws and shook it as hard as he could.

"RRRRRR, *take that, you little hairball,*" growled Barkley.

Back and forth went the dog and the hair. For a while it looked like the hair might win. But by the time Spencer got down from the tree, Barkley was the clear winner. He had eaten Grandpa's toupee.

"You dumb dog!" screamed Spencer. "You ate my grandpa's hair."

Barkley didn't look very good. Grandpa's rug hadn't agreed with him.

Soon he was gagging. Then he was coughing. Spencer gave him a hard

whap on the back. Barkley gave a little shake, and then "Blaaaah," out came the toupee.

"Oh boy," said Spencer as the wig hit the ground.

"Oh no," said Spencer as he picked it up. It was slimy. It was smelly. It was gross.

"This thing is so slippery, Gramps will have to use nails to keep it from sliding off his head."

Spencer had to clean up the toupee. And he had to clean it up before Grandpa got home.

Every day at exactly five o'clock, Grandpa pulled into the driveway. He would park his red truck and march into the house. He'd go straight to his bedroom, take off his hat, and put on his toupee. Spencer had two hours to get that hair de-slimed, de-grimed, and back into Grandpa's bedroom.

Chapter Seven

May This Hairpiece Rest in Peace

Spencer had started around the side of the house when he heard a familiar voice. It was Grandma. She was digging in the flower bed.

"Hold it right there, young man. Where do you think you are going with that dead rat? I can smell it from here."

"What dead rat? I don't have a dead rat." Then Spencer saw that Grandma was looking at the toupee.

"Oh, *this* dead rat," said Spencer. "Barkley caught it in the backyard. You should have seen the fight. It almost killed that dumb dog."

"It probably got a whiff of Barkley's bad breath and had a heart attack. Where are you taking it?" Grandma said.

"Oh, nowhere," said Spencer, sliding the wig behind his back.

"Nowhere is right. I don't want you playing with that thing. You do not know the disgusting places it has been."

"Oh, it was a real nice rat. Before it got in the fight with Barkley it looked good. Good enough to put right on top of your head."

"No one in their right mind would put something as ridiculous looking as that on top of their head."

"Grandpa might," said Spencer.

"Your grandfather looks silly enough in his wig. Even he has his limits. Now, I don't want to talk about it anymore. I will not have a dead critter in my house.

"You take the shovel and that dead rat and go to the back of the yard. Dig a hole and bury it before it starts to smell even worse."

"But Grandma," whined Spencer.

"All right, then, lay it here and I will have your grandfather bury it when he gets home."

"Oh no," said Spencer. "Give me the shovel and I will bury it right now."

"That's my boy," said Grandma as she snipped a flower. "Here, put this flower on the grave. That might make you feel better."

Spencer took the shovel back by the fence and began digging.

"Bury it real deep," called Grandma.

"I'm almost to China now," replied Spencer.

"Just a little deeper," said Grandma.

Spencer finished the hole and dropped Grandpa's toupee in. Then he buried it.

"May this hairpiece rest in peace," said Spencer as he put the flower on the grave.

Chapter Eight

Wash and Dry

After several minutes, Grandma got up out of the flower bed and went into the house. Spencer got right to work.

He started digging as fast as he could. He used his hands so that he wouldn't chop the wig with the shovel.

At last he reached the hair. He pulled it up. It was muddy and a worm was crawling through it. He tossed the worm into the hole and headed for the house.

The screen door slammed behind Spencer as he dashed into the house.

"Who's there?" called Grandma.

"It's me," replied Spencer. "And I don't have any dead animals with me."

"Good," said Grandma. "How was the funeral?"

"It was very nice. Thanks for the flower. I'm going to clean up now," said Spencer as he ducked into the laundry room.

Luckily for Spencer, Grandma was doing a load of wash. He lifted the lid of the washing machine and looked in. It was a load of whites.

"Whites and hair should go great together," said Spencer as he threw the hair in.

He shoveled in a couple of extra scoops of soap just to make sure it would get really clean. Then he saw the jug of bleach. He didn't know what it was for. But, he thought, if Grandma uses it, it must be good. He poured in the entire bottle.

"That ought to do it," said Spencer as he slammed the lid.

Kerplish, kerplish, went the washing machine. Spencer counted the kerplishes. After 212 kerplishes Spencer lifted the lid. He looked in, but there were so many suds he couldn't see the toupee.

He reached in and started fishing things out. The first thing he pulled out was one of Grandpa's T-shirts. "Nope," said Spencer.

Then out came a sock. "Uh-uh," said Spencer as he threw the sock back.

He reached in again and pulled out something weird. "This must be Grandma's," said Spencer. He tried to throw it back in, but a strap wrapped around his wrist. He panicked and started whipping his arm.

"Let go of me! Let go of me!" he cried. Finally, he stepped on it and pulled his arm free.

Spencer got a hanger and used it to pick the thing up. He carefully put it back in the washer. Then he used the hanger for a fishing pole. He wasn't going to put his arm in that washing machine again.

After catching a few more socks, Spencer pulled out the toupee. It was completely covered with suds.

Spencer had to get the toupee dry. He threw the wig in the dryer and set the timer for 20 minutes.

Spencer looked at the clock and then the dryer. This was the longest 20 minutes of his life. Each minute seemed like an hour. At last it stopped.

He opened the door and reached into the hot machine. "Hairy, Hairy, where are you?" called Spencer.

Finally, Spencer got hold of something fuzzy. It had to be Hairy. When he pulled it out, he couldn't believe his eyes. It was fluffy. It was puffy. It was big. And it was really, really white.

"I hope that Grandpa likes this new style," said Spencer.

Chapter Nine

It's a Deal

Spencer put the toupee on his head and looked in the mirror.

"Whoa, if Grandpa doesn't like it, maybe he will loan it to me for Halloween. With this hair, and a big bloody scar across my face, I could scare almost anyone."

Spencer was admiring himself in the mirror when in walked Grandma. She saw Spencer and started to laugh.

"Spencer, what on earth do you have on your head? Why, it's a wig."

Then she stopped laughing. "Oh, Spencer, I hope that isn't your grandad's wig."

"Of course it's not," said Spencer.

"Then where on earth did you get that hair?" asked Grandma.

"A . . . a . . . a hair salesman came by today while you were working in the flower bed. I didn't want to disturb you. You should have seen the hair that guy had. He had a suitcase full of nothing but hair. He was running a special on fluffy wigs, so I bought one. I think it makes me look older. What do you think?"

"I think I smell a rat and I think you are wearing it." Then she looked Spencer right in the eye and said, "Is that your grandfather's wig?"

Spencer looked down at the floor.

"Yes, Grandma. It's Grandpa's hair. I was just playing with it. I was having a little fun, but then it got messy. And before I could clean it up, you made me bury it. I guess that makes it half your fault. I didn't want to bury it, but you made me."

"SPENCER," said Grandma sharply.

"I mean it's every bit, all the way, totally my fault. Do you think that Gramps is going to kill me?"

"Yes, I most certainly do. And I think you just might deserve it."

"Oh, Grandma, I learned my lesson," cried Spencer. "You've got to help me. Don't let Grandpa kill me. If he kills me, I'll never get to go fishing with him again. And if I don't go fishing, I won't be able to catch snakes and sell them for thirty-seven cents each. And selling snakes is the only way I can get enough money to buy you the most excellent present in the world.

"Grandma, you have just got to help me. I promise I'll do anything you say. Please, oh please, help me."

"All right, young man, I'll make a deal with you. You promise to tell Grandpa the truth and I promise to help you if he loses his temper."

"It's a deal," said Spencer.

Chapter Ten

Last Will and Testament

Spencer took the toupee off his head and slowly walked to Grandpa's bedroom.

This is bad, thought Spencer. Very, very bad.

He walked into Grandpa's room and placed the toupee back on its stand. When he turned around, Snickers was there staring at him. He seemed to be smiling.

"You little creep," said Spencer as he kicked in the air. He chased the cat back into the living room. Snickers disappeared under the couch.

Spencer forgot about the cat. He had more important things on his mind. He was thinking of how to escape if Grandpa went berserk.

He walked over and opened a window. Spencer then cleared a path from the couch to the window. He counted the steps as he walked back to the couch.

"It never hurts to have a clear escape route," said Spencer.

Then Spencer heard an eerie sound. It was the screech of the brakes on Grandpa's truck. "This is it," said Spencer.

The screen door creaked as it opened and in stepped Grandpa. It was obvious that he wasn't in a good mood.

"Hi, Gramps," said Spencer cheerfully.

"Hello, Spence," said Grandpa. "I'm sorry about the fishing trip."

"That's OK," said Spencer. "How was your day at work?"

"It was horrible. I thought I was going to kill someone before the day was over."

"You know, Grandpa, there is a law against killing people. Even when they do things they really shouldn't. Why don't you sit down here and tell me some fish stories? Fish stories always put you in a good mood."

"Maybe later, Spence. Right now I just want to get out of my work clothes."

"But Grandpa," said Spencer as he blocked the path to the bedroom. "You look really good in those clothes. I really like that hat. That is one awesome hat. If I were you, I would wear that hat all the time. I would never take it off."

Grandpa took off the hat and put it on Spencer's head. "If you like it so much,

then *you* wear it," said Grandpa, heading for his bedroom.

Spencer put the hat on the table and picked up a pencil and some paper. He went over and sat on the couch.

My last will and testament, Spencer wrote at the top of the paper.

"I leave my snake business to Josh Porter. My brother Jake can have my pocket knife and baseball mitt. I leave my lucky underwear to the New York Mets. If the pitcher wears them, they might win some games. Everything else I donate to the Museum of Cool Stuff. My sister gets nothing. I repeat, nothing."

Chapter Eleven

Truth Time

Suddenly a roar came out of the bed-room.

"MARGE!" yelled Grandpa. "What on earth have you done to my toupee?"

Out stomped Grandpa. He was wearing the fluffy, puffy toupee. His eyes were bugging out and his face was red. He looked ridiculous.

"Spencer, where is your grandmother?" demanded Grandpa.

"I don't know," said Spencer. "Hey Grandpa, did you get some new hair? I really like it. It is very attractive. It makes you look really kind and forgiving."

"If you like it so much, maybe I will give it to you after the trial," said Grandpa.

"What trial, Grandpa?" asked Spencer. His voice was shaking. "You aren't going to kill Grandma, are you?"

"That's a good idea, Spencer. But I think I will just divorce her instead. She has never liked my rug. And now she has gone too far."

"Maybe it wasn't Grandma," said Spencer.

"Who else could have done this?" demanded Grandpa.

"Space aliens," said Spencer.

"Aliens!" shouted Grandpa.

"Grandpa, they were in your room. I

saw them. I tried to stop them, but there were too many for me. There must have been fifty of the little green creeps.

"They were running all around your room. They were in your closet. One was digging in your underwear drawer. And then the leader saw your hair. He started asking it questions. 'Where's your leader? Where's your leader?' When the hair wouldn't answer, he pulled out a laser gun and zapped it. And then he — "

Grandpa interrupted. "Spencer," he said gruffly. "You'd better tell the truth and you'd better tell it now."

"OK, it wasn't space aliens. Would you believe wild monkeys?"

"No monkeys, no aliens. Just tell me the truth."

"All right, it was me. I'm sorry, Gramps. I know I'm not supposed to go in your bedroom, but *that cat*! That cat is evil. He jumped on me and I chased

him. When he ran into your room, I had to follow. You don't want that evil cat in your bedroom. There's no telling what he might do.

"I was looking for the cat when I saw your hair. I just wanted to touch it. But when I touched it, it felt kind of stiff and crusty. I don't mean a bad crusty. It was a real good crusty. It felt so good that I just picked it right up and put it on my head. And when I looked in the mirror, I looked smart. I looked smart and handsome just like you.

"But then it fell on the floor and Snickers came out. That cat really likes your hair. You'd better watch him. He's looking at your hair right now.

"I decided to have a little fun, so I tied some string to it. Then I played Hairball Olympics. You should be real proud of your hair. It won a gold medal. And then it started singing . . ."

"My hair can sing?" asked Grandpa.

"It can if you spin it around real fast.

"And then I invented a great new game. It's called 'Hair in the Air.' You should try it, Grandpa. You twirl it around and then throw it as high as you can. Let me tell you, Grandpa, that hair can really fly.

"But then it got stuck in the tree and I had to rescue it. It was a real scary rescue.

"And then Barkley ate it. Don't worry, he barfed it right back up. But Grandma thought it was a dead rat and made me bury it. I gave it a real nice funeral.

"As soon as I could, I dug it back up. I washed it in the washing machine and threw it in the dryer. When it came out, it was big, fluffy, and totally white. That's the whole truth. I'm sorry, Grandpa. I didn't mean to ruin it."

Grandpa was furious. He was going to

give Spencer the biggest scolding of his life.

Suddenly the bathroom door opened and out stepped Grandma. She was wearing the wildest wig Spencer had ever seen. Her hair was fluffy and puffy. It was much bigger than Grandpa's toupee. And it was ORANGE.

Grandpa took one look at her and started to laugh. He couldn't hold it in. Grandma laughed so hard, a tear rolled down her wrinkled cheek. She took her sweetheart by the hand and they went out the front door. As they left, she turned and winked at Spencer.

Spencer sat down on the couch and let out a sigh of relief. He looked out the window. He could see Grandpa and Grandma in the front yard. They were playing "Hair in the Air."

About the Author

Gary Hogg has always loved stories and has been creating them since he was a boy growing up in Idaho.

Gary is also a very popular storyteller. Each year he brings his humorous tales to life for thousands of people around the United States.

He lives in Huntsville, Utah, with his wife Sherry and their children, Jackson, Jonah, Annie, and Boone.

Here's a sneak peek
at the next

SPENCER'S adventures

#4 The Great Toilet Paper Caper
by Gary Hogg

"Mr. Warner sure gives out a lot of awards," said Josh as the students in Miss Bingham's class began preparing for the final bell.

"Yeah, he's a really nice guy," added Allison. "Somebody should give him an award."

"That is an excellent idea," said Miss Bingham. "We could present him with a special award at the assembly this Friday."

"Awards are nice," said Spencer. "But being famous is a lot better. Why don't we give him a world record. That way we would be giving him more than a certificate. We would be making him famous."

"You heard him this morning," responded Rex. "His ears are big, but they're no world record."

Spencer pulled the *Gigantic Book of World Records* out of his desk. "In this book, there are thousands of different kinds of world records. I'm sure that we can find one for Mr. Warner."

"I like your idea," chipped in Miss Bingham. "But whatever we decide to do must be something in which we can all participate."

Josh's arm shot up. "We could make him the world's biggest banana split. Then we could help him eat it."

Spencer quickly looked up the record in the book. "The current record for a banana split was made with over forty-five thousand gallons of ice cream."

Rex always had his calculator ready. He punched in the numbers and announced, "That means we would each have to bring in one thousand nine hundred and fifty-six gallons of ice cream."

Making the world's biggest banana split was out of the question.

"We could give him the world's smelliest socks. They're my dad's, but I think I can talk him into giving them up," said Alex.

"I think we'll pass on that one," responded Miss Bingham, wrinkling her nose.

"He always wears ties," said Allison.

"That's it," said Josh excitedly. "My mom says that Mr. Warner has the ugliest ties. I'll bet one of them is the world's ugliest."

"Josh," moaned Allison. "I was thinking

that we could make him the world's longest tie."

Spencer flipped through the pages of the book. "The world's longest tie is two miles long," he announced.

"Assuming that we build one hundred feet of tie a day, it would only take us a hundred and five point six days," chimed in Rex, his fingers flying over the calculator.

"Hey, wait a minute," Spencer called out. "Right under ties there is a record that we have a good shot at breaking. The world's largest roll of toilet paper is only six feet four and a half inches tall." Spencer stood up and looked around the classroom. "We could build one bigger than that. And I'll bet that almost everyone in this room has some toilet paper at home."

Some of the kids started to moan. Miss Bingham spoke up. "Now, wait, class.

Spencer might have something here. It's a little unusual, but he's right. We can all get our hands on toilet paper. All in favor of building a record roll of toilet paper, raise your hand."

Everyone but T.J. rasied a hand. He was still dreaming about the world's largest banana split.

"That settles it," said Miss Bingham. "The assembly is this Friday, so let's start collecting paper right away. This is going to be a surprise, so let's keep it as quiet as possible."

"We need a code name for this mission!" exclaimed Josh.

"How about Operation T.P.?" responded Rex.

Soon everyone was chanting, "T.P., T.P."

The excitement was interrupted by the bell. The students quickly put their books away and headed out the door.

TRIPLET TROUBLE

Debbie Dadey and Marcia Thornton Jones

Triple your fun with these hilarious adventures!

Alex, Ashley, and Adam

mean well, but whenever they get involved
with something, it only means one thing —

trouble!

○ BBT90730-X   Triplet Trouble and the Class Trip $3.50
○ BBT90728-X   Triplet Trouble and the Cookie Contest $2.99
○ BBT58107-4   Triplet Trouble and the Field Day Disaster $2.99
○ BBT90729-8   Triplet Trouble and the Pizza Party $2.99
○ BBT58106-6   Triplet Trouble and the Red Heart Race $2.99
○ BBT25473-1   Triplet Trouble and the Runaway Reindeer $2.99
○ BBT25472-3   Triplet Trouble and the Talent Show Mess $2.99

TT796

The Adventures of THE BAILEY SCHOOL KIDS®

Frankenstein Doesn't Plant Petunias, Ghosts Don't Eat Potato Chips, and Aliens Don't Wear Braces ... or do they?

Find out about the creepiest, weirdest, funniest things that happen to The Bailey School Kids!™ Collect and read them all!

☐ BAS43411-X	#1	Vampires Don't Wear Polka Dots	$2.99
☐ BAS44061-6	#2	Werewolves Don't Go to Summer Camp	$2.99
☐ BAS44477-8	#3	Santa Claus Doesn't Mop Floors	$2.99
☐ BAS44822-6	#4	Leprechauns Don't Play Basketball	$2.99
☐ BAS45854-X	#5	Ghosts Don't Eat Potato Chips	$2.99
☐ BAS47071-X	#6	Frankenstein Doesn't Plant Petunias	$2.99
☐ BAS47070-1	#7	Aliens Don't Wear Braces	$2.99
☐ BAS47297-6	#8	Genies Don't Ride Bicycles	$2.99
☐ BAS47298-4	#9	Pirates Don't Wear Pink Sunglasses	$2.99
☐ BAS48112-6	#10	Witches Don't Do Backflips	$2.99
☐ BAS48113-4	#11	Skeletons Don't Play Tubas	$2.99
☐ BAS48114-2	#12	Cupid Doesn't Flip Hamburgers	$2.99
☐ BAS48115-0	#13	Gremlins Don't Chew Bubble Gum	$2.99
☐ BAS22635-5	#14	Monsters Don't Scuba Dive	$2.99
☐ BAS22636-3	#15	Zombies Don't Play Soccer	$2.99
☐ BAS22638-X	#16	Dracula Doesn't Drink Lemonade	$2.99
☐ BAS22637-1	#17	Elves Don't Wear Hard Hats	$2.99
☐ BAS50960-8	#18	Martians Don't Take Temperatures	$2.99
☐ BAS50961-6	#19	Gargoyles Don't Drive School Buses	$2.99
☐ BAS50962-4	#20	Wizards Don't Need Computers	$2.99
☐ BAS22639-8	#21	Mummies Don't Coach Softball	$2.99
☐ BAS84886-0	#22	Cyclops Doesn't Roller-Skate	$2.99
☐ BAS84902-6	#23	Angels Don't Know Karate	$2.99
☐ BAS84904-2	#24	Dragons Don't Cook Pizza	$2.99
☐ BAS88134-5		Bailey School Kids Super Special #1: Mrs. Jeepers Is Missing!	$4.99

Available wherever you buy books, or use this order form

Scholastic Inc., P.O. Box 7502, 2931 East McCarty Street, Jefferson City, MO 65102

Please send me the books I have checked above. I am enclosing $_____ (please add $2.00 to cover shipping and handling). Send check or money order — no cash or C.O.D.s please.

Name _____

Address _____

City_____ State/Zip _____

Please allow four to six weeks for delivery. Offer good in the U.S. only. Sorry, mail orders are not available to residents of Canada. Prices subject to change.

BSK696